Mouse Mischief

Pictures by Jane Pinkney

Story by Margaret Greaves

Libby was so naughty in school that she was kept in.
"Amanda will be flying her kite by now," she said sadly
to herself, "and Pipkin will be fishing for tadpoles."

But soon she was free to join the others.
"Watch me, I'm a juggler!" said Pipkin,
tossing up the ivy berries.

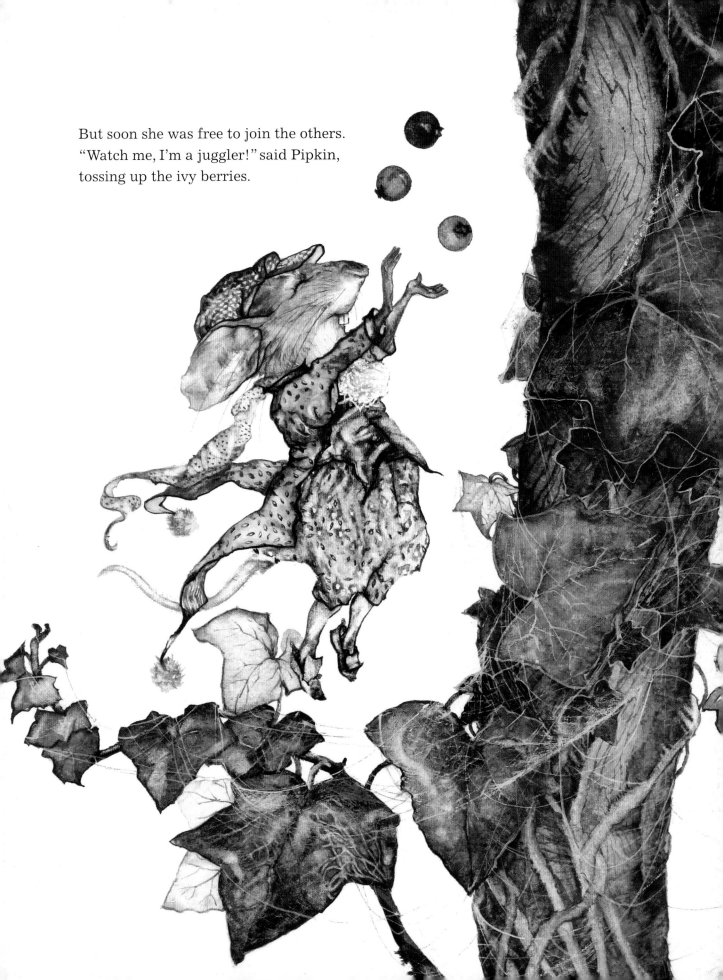

Then a car shot round the corner. "Look out, Pipkin! Run!" shouted Amanda. Pipkin jumped out of the way, but they were all frightened.

"You know we mustn't play in the road," said Libby. "Let's hope no one tells Mother."

"I won't do it again," promised Pipkin. He was very scared too. And they all scampered home as quick as a flash.

Their sister Lucy was to be married the very next day.
She was admiring herself in the beautiful dress she
would wear after the wedding.

"Let's dress up!" said Libby. But soon they were bored.

"I'm going to play marbles," said Pipkin. He let them
go bump from one step to the other.

"And I'll practice my violin in the attic," said Amanda.
But she was only a beginner and made quite terrible noises.

"Whatever is all that noise?" called their mother crossly. "Bumping on the stairs and squealing! I've got enough to do, getting ready for the wedding. Play quietly for goodness sake." The mouse children knew she was really cross.

"Sorry," said Amanda quickly. "I'll look after the babies for a bit if you like?"

The others tried to be quiet and keep out of the way.
Libby teased the china cat with a china mouse.

She put on her hat and coat and she and Pipkin took
turns on the rocking horse.

Then Libby had another idea. "Let's play in the bathroom," she said. "I want to float my boat." But she got in the bath as well, and all the water slopped out.

"Pipkin and I can blow bubbles," said Amanda. "Turn the tap on, Pipkin."

They made beautiful bubbles, but Pipkin forgot to turn off the tap. Soon the bathroom was in a terrible mess.

"Whatever can we do?" wailed Amanda. "Mother will be furious."

"We'll use the big towels to mop it up," said Pipkin. They used all the towels they could find, and the bath mat too. Then they took them out to dry on the washing line. Pipkin swung on the line for fun, but the wind nearly blew him away – and he nearly brought down the line.

"Come in at once, you naughty children!" called their mother. She was very angry. "I can't turn my back for a minute without trouble. If you can't be good you shan't go to the wedding."

That was too dreadful! So Libby helped her to clear up, and make the house pretty for the wedding.

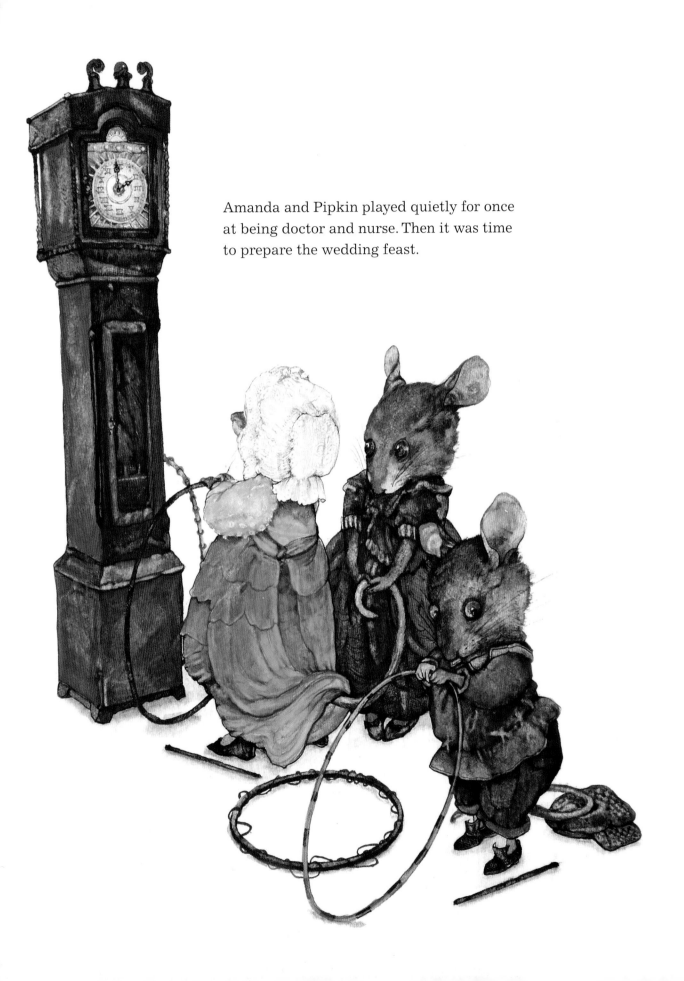

Amanda and Pipkin played quietly for once
at being doctor and nurse. Then it was time
to prepare the wedding feast.

Next day all the grown-up mice wore their best clothes
for the wedding. Lucy was very shy as she and the
bridegroom greeted all the guests.

After the wedding there was a wonderful party in the garden, with crackers and paper hats for all the children.

Pipkin pulled his cracker much too hard and sat down
very suddenly in a bowl of strawberries. Amanda and
Libby were chasing each other round and round the tables.

After the party, Amanda had a good idea. "We'll tidy everything up and give Mother a nice surprise," she said. It was a good idea, until Pipkin started juggling with the plates and Libby dropped a jug and broke it. "It's all gone wrong," said Amanda, and they all wanted to cry.

"Never mind," said their mother, "at least you tried to be helpful. Now it's time for little mice to be in bed."

She tucked them all up, and said goodnight. And the
moon shone down on Amanda and Libby and Pipkin…
all fast asleep and dreaming.

Also available:

The Mice of Nibbling Village

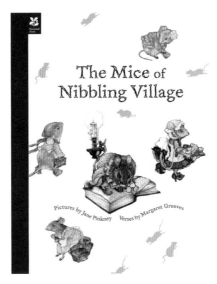

978-1-84365-189-5

This edition first published in the United Kingdom in 2012 by

National Trust Books
10 Southcombe Street
London W14 0RA
an imprint of Anova Books Ltd

A CIP catalogue record for this book is available
from the British Library.

ISBN 978-1-84365-223-6

Printed and bound by Toppan Leefung Printing Ltd, China

10 9 8 7 6 5 4 3 2 1

This book can be ordered direct from the publisher
at the website: www.anovabooks.com